CUENTO
DE LUZ

To my father, Manuel,
who taught me the secrets of the fairground.
- Fran Nuño -

To L. Marina, for giving me your light.
- Enrique Quevedo -

Fairground Lights

Text © Fran Nuño
Illustrations © Enrique Quevedo
This edition © 2013 Cuento de Luz SL
Calle Claveles 10 | Urb Monteclaro | Pozuelo de Alarcón | 28223 | Madrid | Spain
www.cuentodeluz.com
Original title in Spanish: Luces de feria
English translation by Jon Brokenbrow

ISBN: 978-84-15784-20-3

Printed by Shanghai Chenxi Printing Co., Ltd. March 2013, print number 1355-2

FSC
www.fsc.org
MIX
Paper from
responsible sources
FSC® C007923

FAIRGROUND LIGHTS

FRAN NUÑO

ILLUSTRATED BY ENRIQUE QUEVEDO

Once upon a time, my dad took me to a very special fair a long, long way from home. As soon as we arrived, he asked me to wave my hands in the air like a magician so that the lights would turn on or off as I pleased.

"It's amazing!" I shouted with joy.

The first ride we visited was the Witch's Train. Once we got on board, it suddenly soared into the air. A little girl cried, "The witch has left her broom behind, and now she's the train driver!"

Everything looked beautiful from up there.

While on the Bumper Cars, our car left the track
and we drove around the fair for a good while...

...without bumping into anyone, of course!

When we reached the Helter Skelter, we were told
that there was loads of snow at the top,
as if it were the peak of a mountain!

"One day we'll go to the top," my
dad promised. "But we'll have
to make sure we're wrapped
up nice and warm."

We laughed and laughed in the House of Mirrors! Instead of looking fat or thin, tall or short, we were turned into storybook characters!

"Look, Dad! I'm the Big Bad Wolf!"

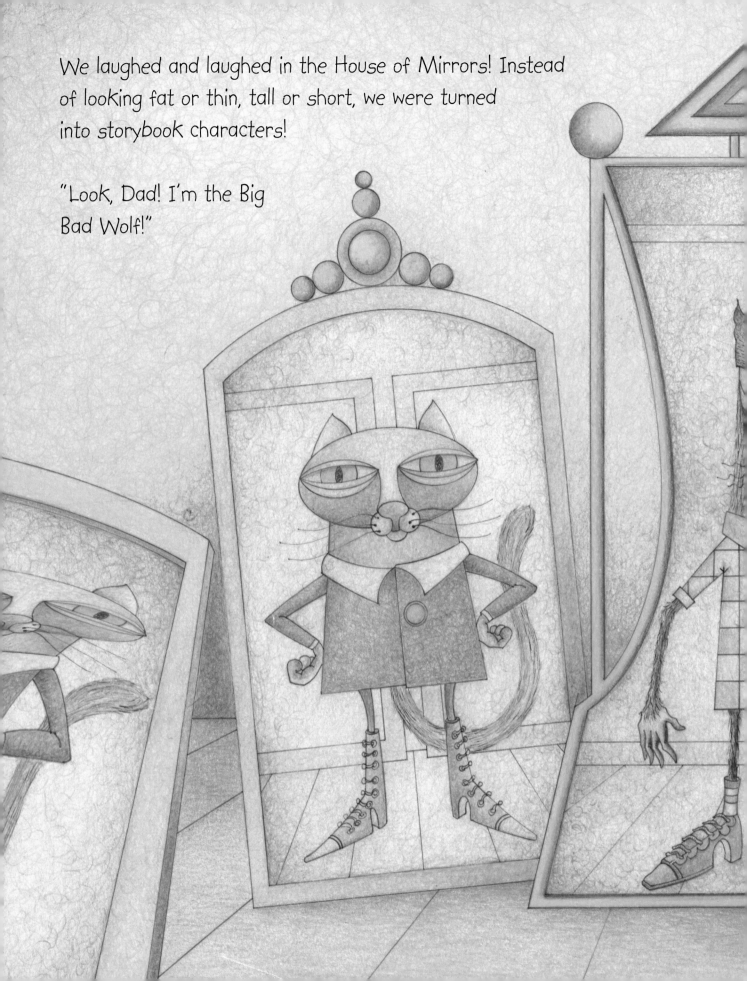

On the Merry-Go-Round, we rode on two very elegant horses. When we got down, my dad told me to look at their horseshoes. What a surprise! They were all scuffed!

"That's because, when nobody's
looking, they run off into the fields to gallop
and play," said my dad
as we headed
toward the
side stalls.

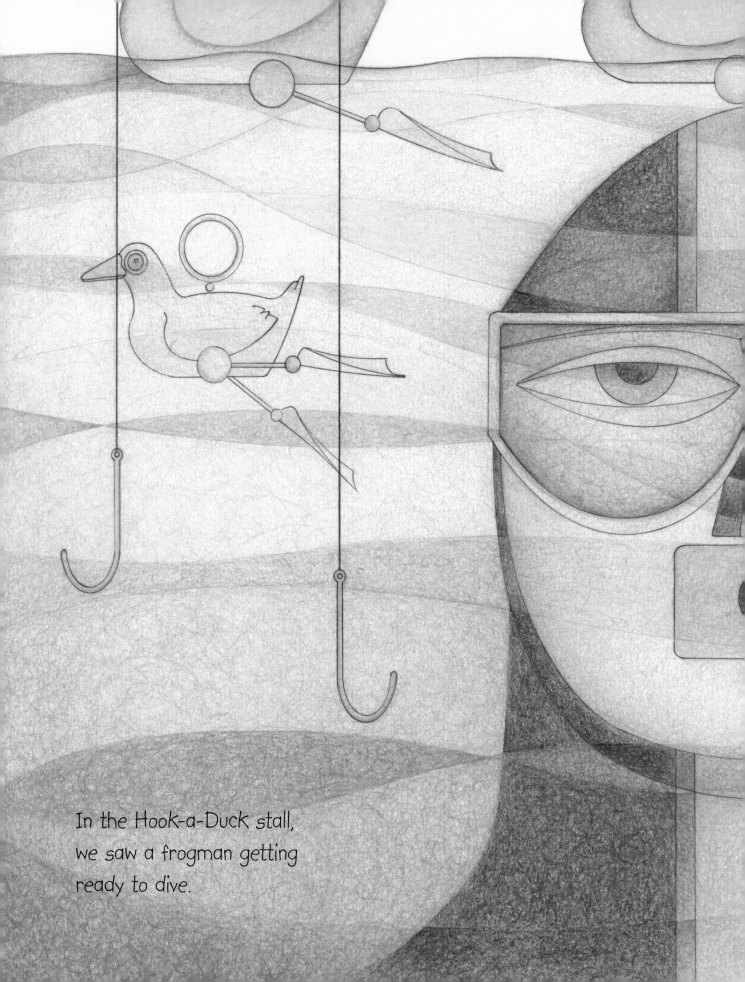

In the Hook-a-Duck stall,
we saw a frogman getting
ready to dive.

"He comes here every day. He's convinced that the duck with the best prize is one that doesn't swim, but instead dives under the water," said the man who ran the stall as he handed us our fishing rods.

I wasn't too sure I wanted to go into the **House of Horrors**, as I'm a bit scared of those kinds of things, but my dad told me not to worry because he'd be right by my side.

I was still **a bit scared**, but we had a lot of fun. On the way out, my dad told me another secret: they say that strange creatures live inside the castle, creatures who are very small and sneaky, who we never see.

The witches and monsters who live there too only have to hear them skittering about and they tremble in

FEAR

I'd never seen a Ferris Wheel like the one
I saw that day. It had the face of a gigantic clock!
We climbed into the seven o'clock car, my dad's
favorite number. When it started to go around,
my dad said to me, "While we're up here, time
stands still for us!"

He was right! When we got off, not
a single minute had gone by!

There were lots of stands selling all sorts of yummy things. We bought some cotton candy, and as I bit into it, I felt something very strange.

Before I could ask him, my dad explained what was happening: "You're eating a piece of cloud, and it's raining sugar in your mouth!"

CANDY

The day was coming to an end, and just as
the lights went out, the fireworks began.
"Just think of a shape, and it'll appear in the sky!"
whispered my dad.

And so, my wish took shape in the sky
over that very special fairground...

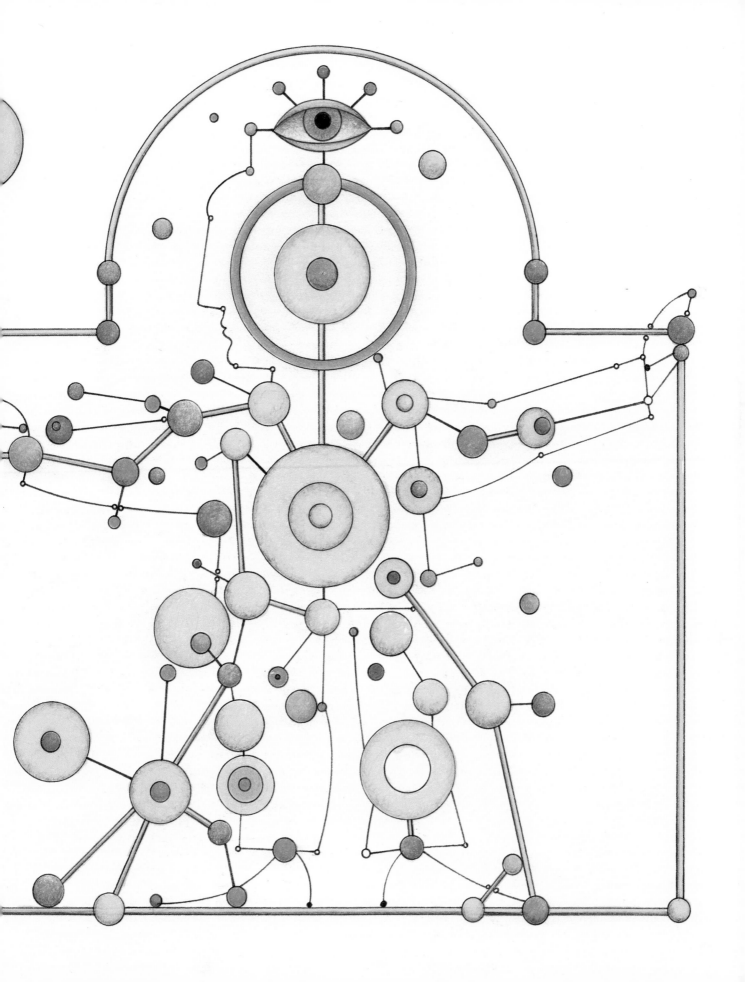